Room on the Broom

For Natasha, Sabrina and Jasmine—J.D.

PUFFIN BOOKS
Published by the Penguin Group
Penguin Putnam Books for Young Readers,
345 Hudson Street, New York, New York 10014, U.S.A.
Penguin Books Ltd, 80 Strand, London WC2R ORL, England
Penguin Books Australia Ltd, 250 Camberwell Road, Camberwell, Victoria 3124, Australia
Penguin Books Canada Ltd, 10 Alcorn Avenue, Toronto, Ontario, Canada M4V 3B2
Penguin Books (N.Z.) Ltd, 182-190 Wairau Road, Auckland 10, New Zealand

Penguin Books Ltd, Registered Offices: Harmondsworth, Middlesex, England

First published in the United States of America by Dial Books for Young Readers,
a division of Penguin Putnam Books for Young Readers, 2001
Published in Great Britain by Macmillan Children's Books
Published by Puffin Books, a division of Penguin Putnam Books for Young Readers, 2003

28 29 30 31 32 33

THE LIBRARY OF CONGRESS HAS CATALOGED THE DIAL EDITION AS FOLLOWS:
Donaldson, Julia.
Room on the broom / by Julia Donaldson ; pictures by Axel Scheffler.
p. cm.
Summary: A witch finds room on her broom for all the animals that ask for a ride,
and they repay her kindness by rescuing her from a dragon.
ISBN: 0-8037-2657-0 (hc)
[1. Witches—Fiction. 2. Animals—Fiction. 3. Dragons—Fiction. 4. Stories in rhyme.]
I. Scheffler, Axel, ill. II. Title.
PZ8.3.D7235 Ro 2001   [E]—dc21   00-045182

Puffin Books ISBN 978-0-14-250112-2

Manufactured in China

Room on the Broom

by Julia Donaldson

pictures by Axel Scheffler

PUFFIN BOOKS

The witch had a cat
and a hat that was black,
And long ginger hair
in a braid down her back.
How the cat purred
and how the witch grinned,
As they sat on their broomstick
and flew through the wind.

But how the witch wailed
and how the cat spat,
When the wind blew so wildly,
it blew off the hat.

"Down!" cried the witch,
and they flew to the ground.
They searched for the hat,
but no hat could be found.

Then out of the bushes
on thundering paws
There bounded a dog
with the hat in his jaws.

He dropped it politely,
  then eagerly said
(As the witch pulled the hat
  firmly down on her head),
  "I am a dog, as keen as can be.
  Is there room on the broom
  for a dog like me?"

"Yes!" cried the witch,
  and the dog clambered on.
The witch tapped the broomstick and
  whoosh! they were gone.

Over the fields and the
   forests they flew.
The dog wagged his tail
   and the stormy wind blew.
The witch laughed out loud
   and held on to her hat,
But away blew the bow
   from her braid—just like that!

Then out from a tree,
    with an ear-splitting shriek,
There flapped a green bird
    with the bow in her beak.
She dropped it politely
    and bent her head low,

"Down!" cried the witch,
    and they flew to the ground.
They searched for the bow,
    but no bow could be found.

Then said (as the witch
    tied her braid in the bow),
"I am a bird,
    as green as can be.
Is there room on the broom
    for a bird like me?"

"Yes!" cried the witch,
    so the bird fluttered on.
The witch tapped the broomstick and
    whoosh! they were gone.

O ver the reeds and the
    rivers they flew.
The bird shrieked with glee
    and the stormy wind blew.
They shot through the sky
    to the back of beyond.
The witch clutched her bow—
    but let go of her wand.

"Down!" cried the witch,
    and they flew to the ground.
They searched for the wand,
    but no wand could be found.

Then all of a sudden
    from out of a pond
Leaped a dripping wet frog
    with a dripping wet wand.
He dropped it politely,
    then said with a croak
(As the witch dried the wand
    on a fold of her cloak),
"I am a frog, as clean as can be.
Is there room on the broom
    for a frog like me?"
"Yes!" said the witch, so the frog
    bounded on.

The witch tapped the broomstick and
    whoosh! they were gone.
Over the moors and the
    mountains they flew.
The frog jumped for joy and . . .

THE BROOM
SNAPPED IN TWO!

Down fell the cat and the dog
and the frog.
Down they went tumbling
into a bog.

The witch's half-broomstick
flew into a cloud,
And the witch heard a roar
that was scary and loud . . .

"I am a dragon, as mean as can be,
And witch with french fries
      tastes delicious to me!"
"No!" cried the witch,
      flying higher and higher.
The dragon flew after her,
      breathing out fire.
"Help!" cried the witch,
      flying down to the ground.
She looked all around
      but no help could be found.

The dragon drew near
      with a glint in his eyes,
And said, "Just this once
      I'll have witch without fries."

But just as he planned
    to begin on his feast,
From out of a ditch
    rose a horrible beast.
It was tall, dark, and sticky,
    and feathered and furred.
It had four frightful heads,
    it had wings like a bird.
And its terrible voice,
    when it started to speak,
Was a yowl and a growl
    and a croak and a shriek.
It dripped and it squelched
    as it strode from the ditch,
And it said to the dragon,
    "Buzz off!–
    THAT'S MY WITCH!"

The dragon drew back
      and he started to shake.
"I'm sorry!" he spluttered.
      "I made a mistake.
It's nice to have met you,
      but now I must fly."
And he spread out his wings
      and was off through the sky.

Then down flew the bird
      and down jumped the frog.
Down climbed the cat,
      and, "Phew!" said the dog.
And, "Thank you, oh, thank you!"
      the grateful witch cried.
"Without you I'd be
      in that dragon's inside."

Then she filled up her cauldron
and said with a grin,
"Find something, everyone,
throw something in!"
So the frog found a lily,
the cat found a cone,
The bird found a twig,
and the dog found a bone.

They threw them all in
    and the witch stirred them well,
And while she was stirring,
    she muttered a spell.
"Iggety, ziggety, zaggety, ZOOM!"

Then out rose . . .

A TRULY
MAGNIFICENT BROOM!

With seats for the witch
    and the cat and the dog,
A nest for the bird and
    a pool for the frog.

"Yes!" cried the witch,
    and they all clambered on.
The witch tapped the broomstick and
    whoosh! they were gone.